This book belongs to

....

igloo

Published in 2010
by Igloo Books Ltd
Cottage Farm
Sywell
NN6 OBJ
www.igloo-books.com

Original story by Igloo Books Ltd.
© Hallmark Cards PLC
Forever Friends is a trademark of Hallmark Cards PLC
www.foreverfriends.com

10 9 8 7 6 5
ISBN: 978 1 84817 700 0

Printed and manufactured in China

Santa Bear

igloo

All the little Bears everywhere have been busy getting ready for Christmas. They wrote letters to Santa, put their letters into envelopes and posted them, with a little help.

They wrote cards to all their
friends and delivered them.

They went ice-skating, and they
built a snowman.

Perfect!

The Bears had fun sledding.

They caught snowflakes.

They went for walks, singing and
dancing in the frosty air.

There was a special Nativity
play with angels.

The Bears sang Christmas songs.

The Bears wrapped their presents
to give to their friends.

They gave each other pretty
flowers and plants.

Finally, it was time for the
Bears to bring home the tree.

The Bears decorated
outside their home with
wreaths, and lights
in the trees.

The Bears decorated inside, too.
They didn't forget the mistletoe!

The little Bears put the Christmas star at the very top of the tree. The Bears' home was almost ready for Santa.

The Bears baked cakes
and cookies and left out
treats for Santa.

They filled the stockings hung from the mantlepiece. It was finally time for the Bears to go to sleep.

Well, almost!

It's time for Santa Bear to deliver all the presents.
He is careful not to forget anyone!

Wake up! It's Christmas morning.
What presents did Santa bring?

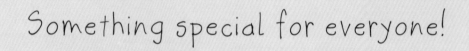

Something special for everyone!

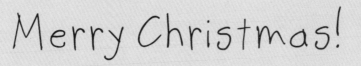

Merry Christmas!